With thanks to Margery

for planting the seed of this idea

Copyright © 1990 by Bruce McMillan. Printed in the United States of America. All rights reserved. Designed by Bruce McMillan. First Edition. Library of Congress Cataloging-in-Publication Data   McMillan, Bruce. One sun : a book of terse verse / written & photo-illustrated by Bruce McMillan. —   p.   cm.   Summary: Describes a day at the beach in a series of terse verses (verses made up of two monosyllabic words that rhyme) accompanied by photographs. ISBN 0-8234-0810-8   1. English language—Rhyme—Juvenile literature.   [1. American poetry.   2. English language—Rhyme.]   I. Title.   PE 1517.M36 1990 811′.54—dc20   89-24625   CIP   AC   ISBN 0-8234-0951-1 (pbk.)

ONE SUN

A BOOK OF TERSE VERSE

WRITTEN &
PHOTO-ILLUSTRATED BY

BRUCE McMILLAN

HOLIDAY HOUSE   NEW YORK

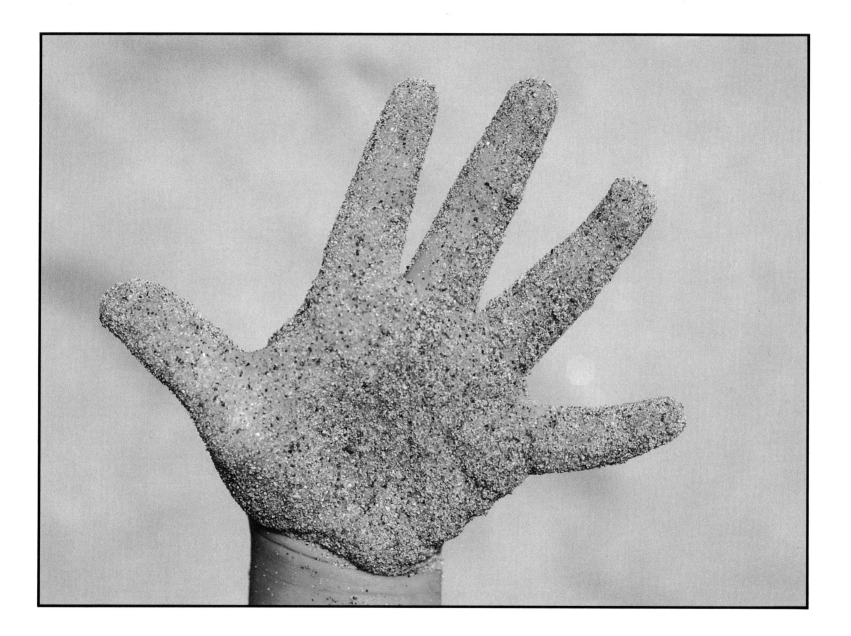

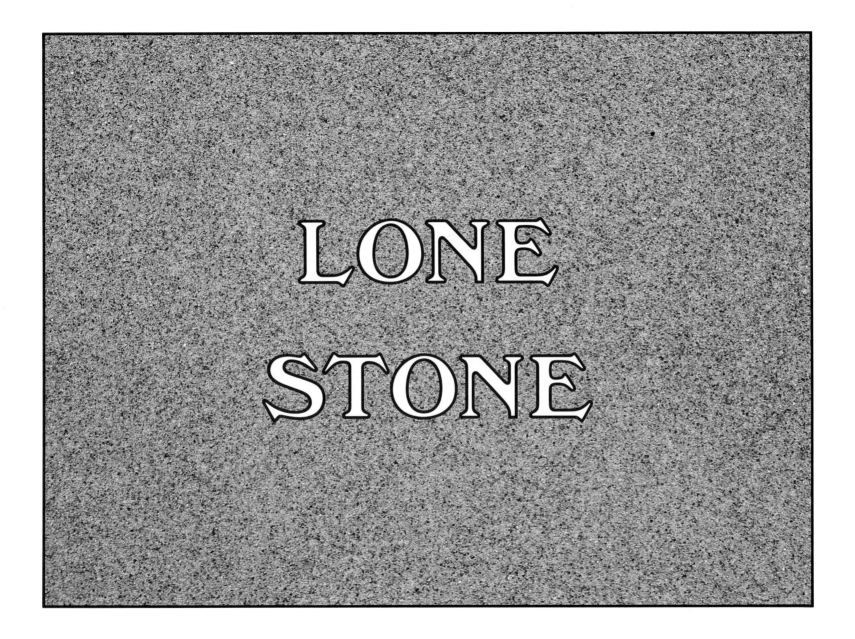

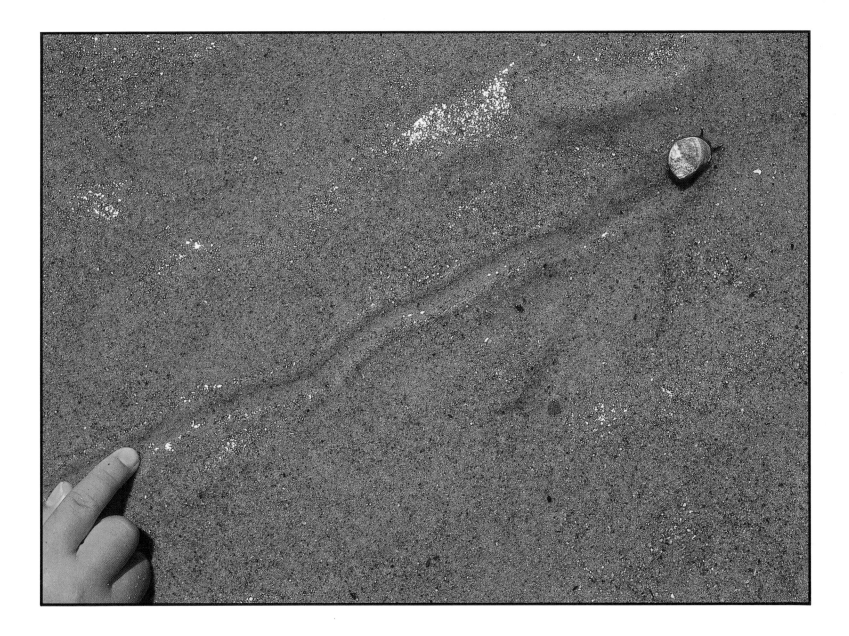

SIX

STICKS

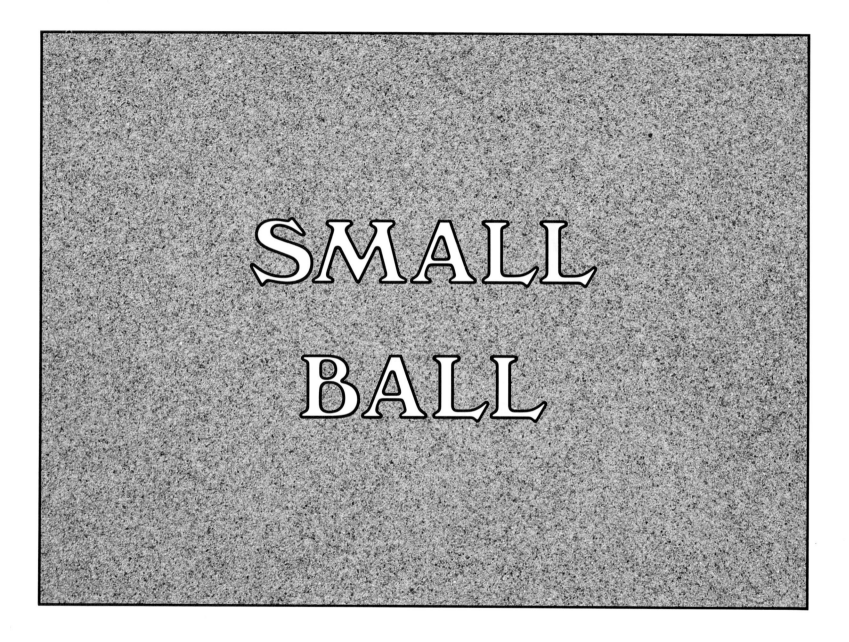

SMALL

BALL

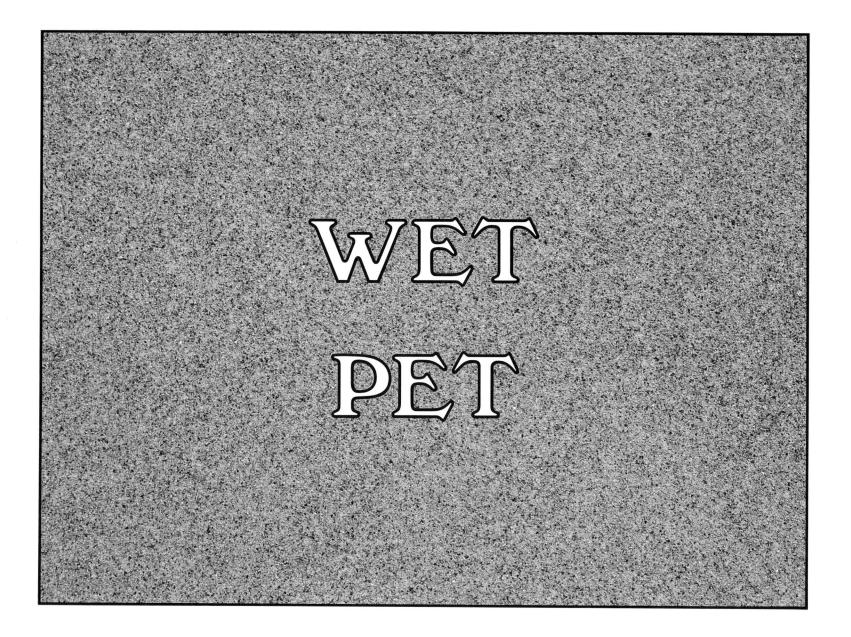

WET

PET

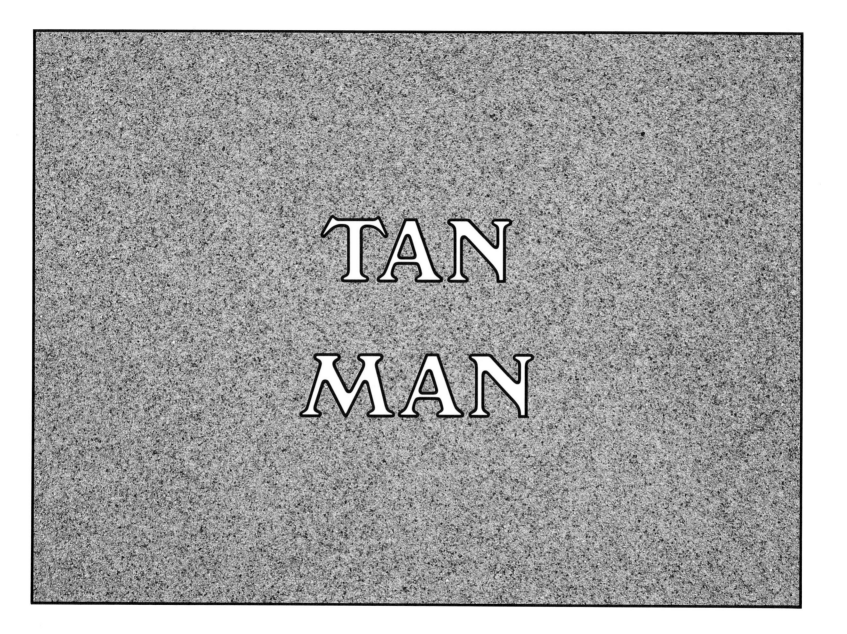

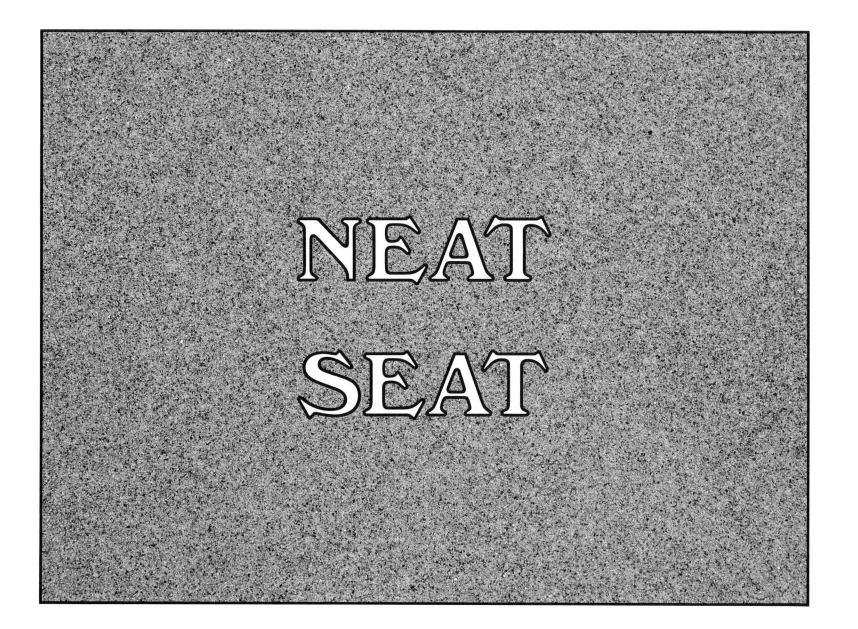

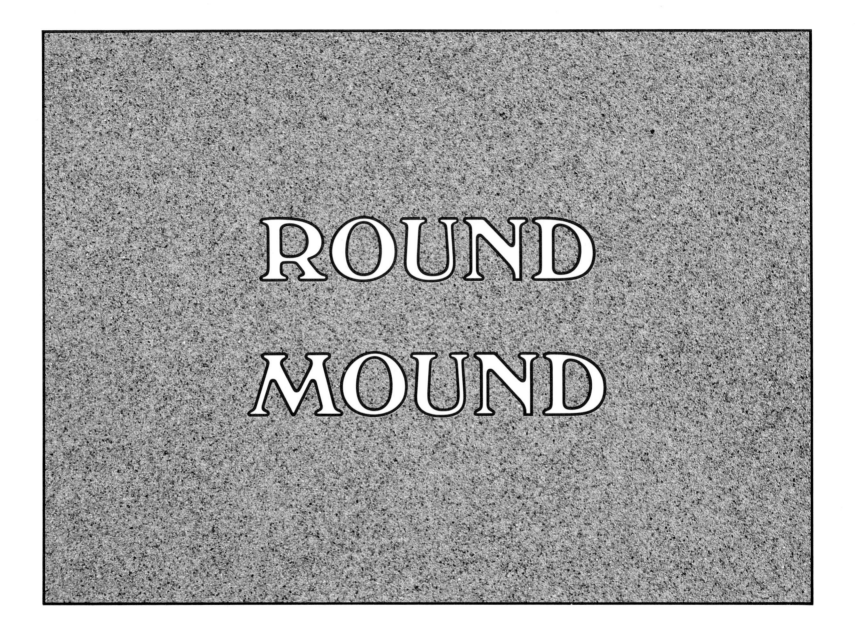

A *"snug tug"* on a *"string thing"* in a *"green scene"*

A terse verse is made up of two monosyllabic words that sound alike. They don't have to be spelled similarly, but they do have to <u>sound</u> alike. Getting children to make up their own terse verses is a delightful and stimulating way of introducing them to rhyme.

One Sun shows a day of play at the beach, but children can make up their own rhyming word pairs about anyplace or anything. For example, children might find a *"big twig"* or see a *"third bird"*! They might still be thinking of terse verses as they fall asleep in a *"red bed"*.

My young friend, Brandon Seavey, was photographed playing at the beaches of York County, Maine. He is the *"one son"* of Betsy, a first-grade teacher, and Stedman Seavey. Also photographed were blue-suited Stacey Bradbury, red-suited Billy Chace, yellow-suited Laura Reid, lifeguard Greg Sturman, and *"wet pet"* Scooby Joyal.

After selecting and coordinating the colors of the bathing suits and props, this book was photo-illustrated using a Nikon F4 with 20mm, 24mm, 50mm, 55mm Micro, 85mm, or 180mm Nikkor lenses; a circular-polarizing filter or blue color-correcting filter; and a reflector to lighten the shadows. The film used was Kodachrome 64 processed by Kodalux.